Praise for *Filled With Purple* . . .

"What's amazing about Melba Burns' writing is the rhythm and the easy, compelling read. For younger women, I know they will want to go out and riot, rebel, and rejoice after reading *Filled With Purple*." *dr. joan e.kole, Artistic Director, AgeQuake Theatres.*

"Dr. Melba Burns' stories are fresh, passionate and peppered with just the right amount of angst. Her light and easy writing style makes them highly enjoyable." *Berny Lucas, award winning children's book author.*

"Melba Burns has done it again! With her unique talent for insightful story weaving, she takes us on quick trips into consciousness of the human condition in a myriad of circumstances. Reading these tales, I feel whole and *so* connected. The characters in *purple* are living scripts that could easily be my own." *Frances Allden, writer.*

"What a wonderful book! The language is so vivid and the challenge to choose life fully will inspire women who read it." *Mary Toth, Life Coach.*

"Burns has a unique style. Character descriptions were excellent, making them come alive. Each should give readers pause for thought; and for many, hope." *Monica Costigan, Memoirist.*

"I was transported to places that I have been and some yet to go. I smiled and laughed, then, reading the next page tears would fall. Melba captures the essence of midlife and holds it up for us to see, taste and feel the pain and the joys – and the *aha* moments that each of us will experience. A worthwhile read for any age." *Bonnie Hope McDonald, www.fromtheheartsolutions.com*

Filled With Purple:

Short Stories & Inspiration for Women

Published by Soul Writes Books
June 21, 2012

Every story in this book is a work of Fiction.
Any resemblance to anyone living or deceased
is purely coincidental.

Melba Burns
219-633 Bucket Wheel Place
Vancouver, British Columbia
Canada V5Z4A7

ISBN 978-0-9689439-6-0

#1 In the Series...

Filled with Purple

© *Dr. Melba Burns*

Published by Soul Writes Books
Vancouver, B.C.
Canada

To my daughter, Donna,

and to all women in those middle years,

to remind you that your spirit will always prevail.

Contents

As she clutched her bag filled with purple,
it was for her
a little bag of mystery,
of life.

Preface

*M*y wish for you, woman in midlife, is that these fictional stories will inspire and empower you to remember your beautiful soul, your inner strength, and your great spirit; no matter what the circumstances or challenges in your life, you can rise above and thrive.

Within this book, two stories were set in times of war: *Wake Up and Roar*, in 1918; and *Morag Quentin*, just after the second World War. In *Not Tonight* and *A New Canvas*, the protagonists evolve from their dark nights of the soul into gaining renewed self-love. Some stories address former relationships that have not worked out. One or two reclaim the forgotten child within. Most reaffirm a woman's identity. *Monday Morning* is about a midlife woman reawakening to her sensuality. *Filled with Purple* is about moving from self-doubt to an exciting awareness of self. The whole book is filled with the mystery of a woman's life in midlife and as she ages.

As you identify with the characters, may you feel their angst as well as their victories, their transformations and their transcendence within your own heart.

Melba Burns

Hurray for Life!

*G*lorious leaves in full flaming colours are tossed and blown in stiff winds. Seasons of time, they curl, then crumple into old gold; tossed off, blown to the ground where they nurture the earth for a future season; gestating through dry cold, then wet; moisturizing their brittleness, to squish into earth and transform within another season.

Rebirth…Renewal.

It is the new we want…

New blouses, new dresses, new jeans, new coats… we toss out our old garments into green garbage bags, scrunch them up into piles, not folds, like when we bought them *new*, when we were excited. When our stuff fades, loses its shape, looks old, it gets tossed out.

What about people?

What about you as you age?

Are you as juicy and passionate as you once were? Still in full flaming red and gold and purple? Is there a stiff wind that will crumple you into the grey and blow you to the ground? Ah, what about your growth? Your acquired wisdom? Was that not one of your goals in life? Would you be so wise if you had not lived this long?

Let's *not* let go yet, nor be squished into oblivion and mashed into wet moss under a tree. Let us choose to stay longer in the flaming red and purple, let our brilliance shine out, dance in our glory – and be passionate as we transform. Let us wave in the breeze and laugh raucously as the wind and the trees and we have a lovely dance. The dance of celebration – of life!

Aging? We may be – but we are not old. We are moving into new stages, and allowing the life force of the Universe to flow right through us.

Hurray for Life!

Wake up and Roar

*T*he year was 1918, and Suzanna Gould sat stiffly on a seaside bench in the late evening sun, clutching the unopened letter from the War Office in her dress pocket. Her betrothed, Joseph Arlington Richards, had been away too long at the war in France, at least that's where one of his last letters had come from, and her heart was like steel in her chest; her belly ached, constantly. Tonight, in honor of their anniversary, the day they met, August 15th, 1916, Suzanna contemplated Joe and their lives together – would they ever be together again?

She'd heard terrible reports from some of the wounded, like her Uncle Thomas, who had been shipped back to England with both legs missing. Now, this formerly peaceful man angrily spewed invectives about the bloody Germans and the god-awful way the men slogged through mud, fought hand-to-hand battles, built mines and were down underground for days. Once, while he was hallucinating, he screamed, "Take that arm out of my face! Get it off, it's not mine!" Oh, could Joe survive this? And if he didn't, what would she ever do?

Here she was, 24, a spinster by some definitions, a sensual woman who missed Joe's arms around her, his tender kisses on her neck and occasionally, down to her breasts. Yes, that one last night before Joe shipped out, they'd gone too far. But was she going to always wonder what it would be like, especially if she never saw him again? They'd promised each other to live their lives together, to travel to Canada and get out of war-torn Europe as soon as they could. But then he was conscripted.

Last October, he'd risen from her bed at 4 a.m., and she'd shyly watched him as he'd dressed. It was while he stood there adjusting his tie on that khaki uniform that she felt her heart silently crack. *Oh Joe, my beloved. Last night you entered my body and today, you take with you a part of me I've never given to anybody, hardly knew was there. My deepest core. My longing to express love as a full woman.*

Not since she was a small girl and had tried to crawl up into her mother's lap when she was nursing her younger brother, had Suzanna felt such pain of loss; for she'd been pushed off and admonished, "Oh you're too big for that now." After that brother, Tommy, came four other siblings, and mother never held her again. So, that 6-year-old little girl decided that she was unlovable, and that she was never going to love anybody. She'd closed up, pretended that her life was fine, staying busy helping mother with the brood, going to school, practicing the piano; living quietly.

Eventually, her hours of practice paid off; her music teacher suggested she perform. So she began playing piano concerts; a life where she could lose herself in her music.

When her elderly Aunt Jane asked if she would move into her sprawling Victorian home to help out in exchange for the accommodation, she was pleased to be out of the family homestead. As her aunt was nearly stone-deaf, she could practice her piano loudly at any time of day or night – but any conversations with her were nearly impossible. So, although she loved her music, she still felt lonely.

It was only when she met Joe and he looked at her with such adoration shining out of his eyes that she felt the surge of love return to her heart.

She'd all but given up those thoughts of being loved by any man. She was too tall, too slender, *skinny* her mother called her, and her jaw was too strong for a woman. Her father always said that she looked very determined all the time. Her nose was a bit too small for her large face, and her red hair was too curly; why it sometimes flew around her face if she didn't put it back into a bun.

But while glancing at herself in the mirror, she began to notice her eyes, and see the tiny gold specks in the green, trying to see what Joe called "beautiful." Were they really? Well, she loved it that he saw that in her. With him, she felt "pretty" of all things. She, pretty. She'd never dreamt it. But Joe told her she was.

So this evening, she had on that beige lacy dress that he liked, the one she'd worn at the concert where she'd met Joe, at Bluvey Hall. The way he'd looked at her that evening and asked if he could escort her home, she just knew she had blushed and all of her freckles had most likely deepened into a burnished orange, popping out past the powder she tried to camouflage them with. But he hadn't seemed to mind.

All she remembered about that walk home was that he took her arm and linked it with his and she just couldn't stop smiling; thought her cheeks would never stop holding that smile.

For the very first time ever, as she stole glances at this soft brown-haired man with the too large nose and the full lips, the lean cheeks and a too-prominent Adam's apple, she felt tiny – yes, he was even taller than she— and truly cared for. She could see it in his deep blue eyes, the way they shone out to her. And she heard an impassioned man speaking of his vision to become a builder of fine homes in Canada.

He was a stone-mason here in Lancashire, and he wanted to take this skill to another country too. He'd been reading about Canada, and had the urge to go there. His mother had died the previous year and his father wasn't around much, and being the youngest in the family, there really wasn't any reason for him to stay.

Suzanna leaned back against the bench and stuffed that ominous prickly letter back into the pocket of her ankle-length dress, wiped her wet hands on the soft material. She didn't want to deal with any bad news. No, it was too painful to even think about right now. Later she would open it and find out what it was. She'd heard of these War Office letters; they destroyed lives. Joe was alive – had to be. She wasn't going to believe anything else.

She closed her eyes and prayed.

Then, she began to hear a voice rising within her, almost a roar, almost a command, urging her to do something. What? What could she do? She was alone, and her beloved was in France, and tonight all she could do was sit there and pray, one tear escaping out of the corner of her eye, slipping down her cheek until it eased down onto her neck. She didn't wipe it away.

But she shook her head and sat up, opening her eyes and staring out to the dark blue sea, now frothing with white caps. Something came over her, some inner strength; the kind she sometimes felt before she would play Rachmaninoff's Concerto in C# minor; an energy that filled her up and brought her back.

Standing up and leaning into a strong breeze, the gusts whipped the silk of her dress tight against her legs and loosened the bun from the back of her head, her hair flying around her face. Suddenly, she was drenched with perspiration, burning hot, like there was a fire in her. As if possessed, the voice in her took over: she raged and roared into the wind, louder than she'd ever done, louder than Mrs. Hancock who sang like an opera star, louder than Mr. Adams when his leg was broken under a lorry, louder than her uncle's ranting and ravings.

"No, I will not lose you, Joe! Come back to me. I love you! You hear that, I l o v e you!"

Her words carried far out to sea, into pockets of the earth never before touched by her, into Canada, and Germany–and into France, into the trenches there. Reverberating words by her breath, they were cast and then breathed in by others. Her words went out and were heard.

Then she turned and strode back across the high field, her hand clutching the letter in her pocket, willing its contents into the shape she wanted. Head held high, she walked into the grand imposing Victorian home, up the stairs and into her own room. She closed the door. The bed creaked as she sat upon it. With cold trembling fingers, she opened the letter. Now she was prepared to know. Now she could take it. "Wake up and Roar!" That's what that voice had shouted at her, now she remembered.

The letter said: *This is to inform you that Joseph Arlington Richards, was wounded in action and will be returning to London's Mercy Hospital, on August 17th.*

With a huge sigh, she bowed her head, closed her eyes, and whispered, "Thank you, thank you, thank you..."

Ain't That Good Enough?

I am in awe of all the green around my face, my black face. I am 89 years young, and I sit by the fires – burnin' away the pain of my youth. Yeah, remembering all that purple passion in the lettuce leaves, and all those blue tendrils of my hair running down my back, all the way to this earth and into the dank damp soil.

Oh, I loathe letting go. It's hard to do. But who really cares anyway? Them shining Appalachians over there soothe my soul, and I jest sit against my favorite rock and pray. Pray for my sons and daughters who went to their cherry ways long ago – until my teeth fell out from gnashing their indiscretions against my lower jaw, and aching my bones there. 'Till my ol' man could hardly hear me anymore.

Well, his beard covered his ears and the old bugger didn't know how to even make me happy – if you knows what I mean – you know, in that womanly way, the one that loosens up your pelvis and makes you walk different. You know, when you feel your cheeks raising up to your eyes and you know your mouth is grinning all by itself. Nope, he was already wizened up before his days of so-called wisdom.

He thought I was his beloved property that he could boss around, tell me where to sit, who to be with, whether to cook up chitins or corn; all that stuff. Truth be known, he was the only one who thought he was boss, if you get the picture. I mean, our babies came outa me, and scared him half to death. Oh, he pretended he knew what to do 'round those little ones, but when each babe was suckin' at my tits, it made him so nervous, he smoked his ol' pipe a lot – yep, hid behind that pipe till all he could do was sit and suck and get sour and tell the world to shut up. And he stopped looking at me square in the eye – and guzzled his moonshine too.

Well, I says to him, "Now Henry, you jest shut your mouth, 'cause nobody's listening." So he did. But he kept on with that moonshine for a lotta years.

A long time later, I laid him to rest – just over there under that apple tree. You know, I sorta miss the old bugger. Resting there too are three of my sons – killed by the white man's guns, and gin, in the late 50's. Laid out on the curb, one of them. Lordy Lordy…

The rest of 'em are far away, too far. Even my little girl – she's gettin' on now; guess she's 'bout 55. Up north with all the others.

Well, I think I'll stay here and rest awhile and watch the moon turn blue. Why, I might even dance on the pine needles like I sometimes do, and shout at the ol' lady up there, and bay at the wolves. It's okay. Yep, I got *me!* And what the hell, ain't that good enough?

A Master-Presence

A s a mature student studying journalism, I had wanted a good teacher for a long time – but on Hastings at Gore Street? It wasn't a great part of town.

I looked at the older man with ravaged gullies in his red and whiskered complexion as he stood there with Spare Change magazines in his hands. I handed him a dollar and he stared at me with oceanic green gray eyes, eyes so deep I knew I'd drown in them if I didn't tear my gaze away; hypnotic they were. I focused just below them and noticed the gray, nearly black puddles underneath, and then, his very large nose with huge nostrils, and dark little hairs in those caverns. I didn't like that nose so I zoned in on his dark black brows that curved in a V; and up above those, three deep gouges across his forehead, as if he'd been whipped. His hair was the color of mud, flecked with gray and it receded on both sides of a very pointed widow's peak; giving him an aristocratic air. His ears were tight to his head, his jaw firm, although his neck was slightly turkey-wattled. He had a metallic odor about him, like something inside him wanted to come out. It permeated his whole body; made me sick to be so close. So I backed away. Besides, he may not have had a bath for a couple of days. His old corduroy jacket was stained on one sleeve, his red and black plaid shirt open at the collar, showing a blotchy clavicle and a huge Adam's apple. As he lit a cigarette, I noticed his nails were rimmed with black and slightly bitten. But as he spoke in his broken English, I had to listen.

"You think you are better than me, no?"

"Whatever makes you think that?"

"I know you. You come down here to feed the hungry, the poor – then you go back to your big house in... Kerrisdale, yes, and you tell your friends you are, ah... *contributing*. Then you sleep better at night. No?"

"For one thing, I don't live in that area – I live in Kits. For another, I don't come down here to feed the hungry and the poor." He was making me uncomfortable so I clung onto my purple Giorgio purse, the one with the shoulder strap I can wrap around my body – and I began to walk away.

"Where you go? Cannot take truth, eh?"

I stopped in my tracks. "I told you, I'm not doing what you think I am....I'm trying to write a paper for my journalism class, so I'm doing research."

"Oh, isn't that nice now... gonna *write* about the hungry and poor. Well make sure you get the stories right. Poor bastards do not want to be, ah, how you say, misrepresented now, eh?"

"I don't intend to misrepresent anybody."

We stood there on that sorry sidewalk, staring at each other like boxers in a ring. I wanted to get in my little Toyota and get out of there.

Professor Giles had sent me down here to get a story for my third year class in journalism, but I hadn't thought it would be like this. Me, Bonnie Tuttle, 39, too old to be scrapping with a man who lives on the street; I was just doing my best to get through the program at UBC, and sure didn't need this hassle. Besides, I had to meet Bruce in an hour and didn't want to be late. We'd just started dating, and you know when you're nearly forty and your biological clock is ticking away, you sure don't want to keep potential fathers away. Bruce was a good man, knew what he was after and went for it. Why, he was working on a book – talking to Random House about it. I knew I could learn a lot from him.

"Listen," I said, "I can't talk now... I've got to meet somebody and..."

"Oh sure..." His voice was stronger now. For a man of about 60, maybe older, he had a lot of energy in that voice. Fog horn energy, raspy – but when he blew that horn, one took notice. I shuddered and faced him head on. Had to. Those eyes were even deeper now, drawing me in. You know when you start wading into the ocean, and want to go real slow, and then suddenly the bottom drops out and you're soaked, and, well..

...I agreed to a coffee with him at Lorraine's cafe.

We sat across from each other: he, lighting up another Export, and calling out in a real macho voice like he owned the place to the waitress over behind the white-gray counter, "Hey sweetheart, make it two javas. Steaming hot and fresh!" Me, I was trying not to notice the dirty chipped linoleum and the grunge-gray curtains – or the old reprobate over there in the corner who looked sound asleep and about to fall under the table.

The blond gum-chewing waitress came over with coffee. "You never change, Servascio... Here ya go. You'd think you were master of the world the way you talk."

Servascio laughed and patted her bum. "I am, Lorraine, my darling; you know that." She seemed to welcome his touch. I didn't even ask; it was their life, not mine. I was leaving as soon as this coffee was drunk. Well, little did I know about this man. He began to talk...

"The Croats are not the victims over there you know. I come here four years ago, work hard to be mechanic, to get a truck. My father used to take me in his truck with him when I was just how you say... snot-nosed boy. We built trucks. Many. I grew up helping Father build them. But they shot him...and my mother... as they were walking across the town square..." His voice quavered.

I just sipped my coffee and waited. He carried on...

"...And I knew *then* I would not stay. But when the blood is running in the streets and the people are terrified and the babies are all crying and even the little children in the streets are playing with real guns, you cannot do much." He blinked fast, stared at the ceiling, then back at his coffee, slowly stirring more cream into it – shuddering, involuntarily.

Softly, I asked, "So what did you do then? How did you get here?"

"After the funeral, I say farewell to my aunts and uncles – you know, just like I will see them next week. But I know I am going. And then, I go see my woman at her house. Marina." His voice lingered on the syllables of her name, like silk. "I ask her if she will come with me. Be with me. She is horrified. Says she cannot leave...reminds me of the cancer in her mother, talks of Roul, her son in nearby city, who sometimes visits. She could not do it." His ocean eyes are swimming now.

"But didn't you love her?"

"Love – of course I did. We both cried... But is one to give up their *soul* for that?"

All I managed to croak out was, "Soul?"

I thought of Bruce. Of Joseph, the one before him. Of Clive. Of Anthony. Of all the times I gave myself up for them. With Joseph, I had just written a script and was going off to Los Angeles with it – but he needed me; can't even remember why. I didn't go... couldn't leave him. With Clive, he said he supported my writing, but when I had a story published, he stopped calling. And Anthony, he thought my writing was a fad and that I'd grow out of it. He was a business man who *never* thought about his soul.

I looked at this man across the table, lifted my cup to my lips and then the damned thing dropped, and spilled all over the table. Soul, I thought, *where was mine lately?*

"Soul. Is that not what life's all about? Looking after it, trusting it knows what it wants..."

I was drowning in those eyes. No, as he looked at me something kept me afloat. But here I was, down here too deep. I called over to the waitress. She wiped up the table, then poured more coffee and put a basket of pretzels on the table. I stuffed my face. My belly hurt. I was starting to sweat. "So what'd you do?"

"I hopped freighter… and here I am. But life is hard here… You do not know stories of these people on this street. I drive cab. I work in gas station too… and four months ago I hurt back when car fell off the hoist. My friend says I should take money from your government… until my back is better… but I cannot do that. "

"Why not? Isn't that what it's for? To help people out?"

"I am able-bodied man. Only 48 years old. I do what I can. Cab is not bad….

"Why, when social assistance is there for people, would you not apply for it? Or take it? Why would you rather put out your hand for assistance to somebody in the street?"

He bristled and his mouth tightened. "I am selling those magazines. There is pride you know. Perhaps you do not know what this means. But I have that. I did not come here to take from your government. I will heal soon. In meantime, some friends help me out. Like Lorraine here. Free eggs, bacon, coffee on house. We help each other. Life is about that – yes?"

Glancing at my watch, I realized I'd missed Bruce. It didn't seem to matter. But I was filled up and wanted to go

– just anywhere, to digest it all. I put out my hand and he shook mine with a strong grip. "Thank you," I whispered. "You taught me a lot today."

He smiled a broken-metaled smile, and with two fingers, tapped his chest: "As long as you do not forget this. Your soul, eh?"

I placed my hand on my chest. No, I wouldn't forget. It was darned well time to remember it. To remember *Me*.

I made my way to my Toyota, climbed in and started the engine. As I drove past the restaurant, I saw him just walking out. His back was stooped over, he walked slowly, but with such a sense of pride – I knew that just as Lorraine the waitress had said, I *had* been in the presence of a master.

Morag Quentin

*S*he stumbled up the old creaky steps to her large sprawling clapboard house, the one she'd called home for the past eleven years; the one they'd fixed up together. But as she dragged her leaden feet across the porch, slowly creaked open the old screen door and heard it thwack against the frame, her feet squeaking along the old polished wooden floors and into the bright kitchen, now, this god-awful morning, it was suddenly just a house. How was she going to get through this?

Her hand lifted the kettle, took it to the sink and filled it with water. Her backside slumped down heavily onto the pine chair to wait. For what? She didn't care. For something – call it that screeching kettle; to mother her, to tell her to make tea, to move slowly and sip it carefully so you don't burn yourself. Don't move; as if some voice inside of her were whispering, *You will survive; other women get through this.*

But as she tried to raise the hot tea to her cold lips, tears scalded at the edges of her eyes and down her cheeks. Her arms jerked and her stomach and chest were pumping, so hard, the cup flew out of her hands, and she bent over and held herself, wailing, falling to the linoleum floor, the very one *he* had installed just one month ago. She curled up into a fetal position, holding her body, holding it like she would her favorite golden retriever who'd been hit by a car, holding it together so its limbs wouldn't fall from the trunk. Then she heard the guttural sounds spewing from her, as if they were disembodied; sounds like an animal, sounds that surprised her but she couldn't quell. Sounds of such grief; low and long and languid; sounds that one needs to make to heal.

Much later, as Morag stared at her disembodied image in the bathroom mirror, the round face even more puffy, that long brown-gray streaked hair tumbling out of the French braid, those gray-blue eyes still welled up with tears. Tremors shook her shoulders. Shivering, she reached for an old plaid shirt at the back of the door; his. She slipped it on anyway, covering her simple printed rayon dress – the one he always liked; used to say it made her look sweet and feminine. She knew that it covered her slight tummy, still not firm from Jenny's birth five years ago. She rubbed her belly slowly then let her hands slide up to her full breasts, placing her palms over them. He wouldn't be touching these breasts anymore. She closed her eyes to the mirror, shook her head and ambled into the bedroom; theirs – till this morning.

She lay down on the double bed covered with the green satin quilt, embroidered with tiny white daisies. Today, it was too bright; the lacy curtains blowing slightly in the breeze were too happy; they should stop moving – just like her world.

She flipped one edge of the quilt over her as she lay on *her* side of the bed, moved her hand in an arc over to *his*, then brought it back to her stomach, rubbing the sudden ache. Eyes slammed shut, she turned towards the wall, wishing with all the un-shattered self that still dangled within her that the sun would stop shining, that the sweet scent of blossoms on the apple tree wouldn't waft in like that – wishing she could stay where she was, forever.

Wishing she had never loved him.

Had she not shown him? Had she not cooked his favorite meals, or gotten up with him for breakfast? Or been there when he wanted to talk? Had she not been pretty enough? Good enough? Had she not succumbed to him when he'd wanted her?

What the hell had he wanted anyway?

She stayed in that painful black fog for a long time.

Three hours later, Morag was outside in her garden; bending over, yanking out the damned weeds with a vengeance. Muttering out loud to the blackened earth as if that were the problem, *"Damn it, damn it, how dare you do this to me!"*

Tears still streamed down her dirt-streaked face while she raked the black soil with the claw tool, dug in deep and squeezed and twisted her strong right hand around any old green shoot that didn't belong there with the red and purple tulips. No, she would wring the necks of those damned invaders, wrench out any goddamned thing trying to steal the life force from what she had so preciously planted. Nothing was going to destroy what she had envisioned. Nothing or *nobody*.

But how was she going to make ends meet? In 1945 there weren't many jobs for women. It wasn't even thought proper for a woman to work. But when she saw Jenny and ten-year-old Will scooting up the road, lunch buckets in hand, she knew she'd have to do something. What that was, she had no idea. But she was a *feisty broad* wasn't she? That's what he always used to tell her, long before this morning…

… Long before he'd driven his old truck up into the driveway and had just sat in it, like something was wrong. So she'd gone out to greet him, but he wouldn't get out of the driver's seat. When she'd asked what was wrong, he avoided her eyes. Finally, he climbed out, stood there on the unpaved driveway, fiddling with his keys, sheepish, looking like a dog that had just peed on the rug. Nibbling on his bottom lip, he ran his fingers through his dark brown hair, and took a deep breath. Then confessed: where he'd been and why he'd spent so many nights away… *there was this special woman… he absolutely had to be with her and… he was sorry… but he just couldn't help it… and she'd asked him to move in with her…*

Still planted there in the garden, she muttered out loud, "Oh Morag, what now?"

Then, she stood up straight, rubbing her aching back. Her children were running to greet her with delightful innocence written all over their faces. She forced her mouth to move into a smile. Hard as that was, she knew that they depended on her.

She had to trust; in something; in herself. Yeah, she was a *feisty broad*. Maybe she'd turn the place into a rooming house. That's what *he'd* always said, that when the men returned from the war they would need places to live, and there were plenty of rooms in this old house.

She'd get through this time. They all would…somehow.

Not Tonight

*S*he sipped her nearly-white coffee at *The Muffin Break*, coffee she had given up three years ago, but what the hell, who cared. Soon, it wouldn't even matter.

She sat there at her table-for-one that January, her brown eyes, heavy-lidded and downcast, her stylish purple coat draped over the back of the chair. Although her skin was slightly freckled from too much sun in her younger years, her dark hair, now streaked with gray and pulled back into a long braid, she had a dignity about her; even at 52, Peggy McDonnell was still attractive. But she didn't know that. She watched the Saturday evening traffic zip by, *probably on their way to important events*, she thought. She remembered that old feeling; picking up loved ones, driving off to a party or a concert, or sitting close and holding hands in a darkened movie theater.

The restaurant door opened. A cold breeze wafted across her tense face as a man in his forties entered. She glanced up; then down again to her important dinner, a blueberry muffin and soup. Her mind whirred like the nervous laughter of the four year old boy sitting over there with his mother, punctuating guffaws with kicks against the beige wall. The man ordered his dinner and sat away over in the corner. He never even saw her there.

Where had it all gone?

How had she arrived here?

Leaning back, she glanced at the ivy plants over her head, artificial ones of course. Nothing was real anymore. The little boy whined for attention, but Mom was preoccupied with the newspaper. Still, she heard her whisper, "I'll show you the funnies..." That old bribe...

"I'll show you the funnies if you come with me, little girl," the man had said, so many years ago. It didn't seem to matter how many, – the memory was as clear as yesterday. He drove her down through the dark park, her heart thumping, and what he'd shown her wasn't funny at all. No one heard. No one came – except the man.

She stuffed a large piece of muffin into her mouth, gagged for a second, then leaned back; trying to unwind that same old horror movie.

Memories of other men flitted through her head; old films, black and white; George and Henry and Ben. And Joe... With him, it hadn't worked. He'd spoiled her with beautiful dresses and shoes and presents from all over the world. But she knew the presents always meant, *"Now what'll you give me?"*

The cash register crackled. Two young men with long hair left the restaurant. Anne Murray warbled into her brain, *Could I Have This Dance For The Rest Of My Life?* Sure, they always said that. Ben used to sing it to her when he couldn't even dance. But his loving was so great it hadn't mattered. Then it changed. *She* came along. Younger, prettier, sexier, even had money. Who could blame him?

Her old blue Dodge was glistening in the night light outside. Old reliable; twenty years old it, still ran. Longest relationship she'd ever had. And every time she climbed in, the old black, fuzzy slip-covers just slipped around her back and legs like they were part of her skin. Supported her. Nothing else did. Nobody did.

Not Mathew or Brent. They'd both left. Most sons hang around for awhile, at least until they're married or with a woman – but they hadn't. One lived in Florida. The other, she wasn't even sure. Well, who cares? Two less to notify afterward.

She walked up to get another cup of coffee. Her stomach usually hurt when she poured this hot stuff in. But there wasn't much time left so it wouldn't matter.

A good looking gray haired Oriental man came in, bought his perfect muffin and left. He never even glanced over at her. They'd all stopped looking a few years ago. Before, they would "hit" on her every time she sat alone in a restaurant. Now, not even a glance. She was invisible.

Her hands were numb. The coffee cup clattered out of her hands, spilled its guts all over the table. She was beyond blushing. The waitress, a young pretty girl in her twenties, cleaned it up.

"Are you okay?" this young girl with the long blond hair asked.

"Me?" She glanced up just long enough to see LUCY on her name-tag.

"Yeah, you look... well... sad, so sad. You okay?"

"Fine."

Lucy paused, pressing the cloth between her hands, then timidly stood in front of her table and began to speak; slowly. She cleared her throat and then said it: "My brother died three months ago."

"Oh? Sorry to hear that." Peggy's voice sounded flat, even to herself.

"Nobody would've guessed he was down. They found him in his room... the chair tilted... hanging by his tie... his favorite red tie."

Peggy shuddered, then struggled to slip her coat around her shoulders. Lucy helped her; draped the purple wool onto her like a shroud. Peggy's head wobbled heavily, "I'm sorry."

"Yeah... me too. It never goes away. I miss him so much. I wish he'd talked to us... before."

Peggy inhaled deeply, then pursed her lips and slowly blew out as she fumbled in her purse. With shaky hands she drew out her blue leather wallet, and opened it up to the pictures she carried. "See these? My sons."

The young girl studied the photographs. "Nice looking, both of them."

"Yes… take after their father. You ever visit your Mom?"

"Not too often."

"You young people never do." She got up to go.

Lucy stayed there, in her path. "I'm sorry… sorry that some of us don't."

Tears flowed then, all down Peggy's cheeks. *Damn it.* She reached for her sunglasses.

"No..." Lucy spoke with a vehemence that surprised even herself, "It's good. Don't hide them. My Mom never cried when Mickey died and now she's like stone."

She stood there, staring into this young woman's face. So alive that face; look, tears were welling up in *her* eyes.

"Please, your sons care. They... maybe they forget."

This girl was so filled with life, and some kind of niceness, that Peggy had to inhale very deeply and touch her own chest. She nodded. *Maybe they do forget.*

She shook the young hand. It was warm. She handed her $5, murmured, "Thanks," then left. She turned once as she walked by the window and a slight smile began to spread across her face as she caught Lucy's eye.

She got into old faithful, Bessie, revved the engine, felt the black fur enfold her, and drove into the busy street. It was then she decided: *No, I won't do it tonight..*

Out loud, she spoke to her little Dodge, "I think I'll see a movie. And maybe tomorrow I'll walk in the park... maybe my neighbor Rose will join me."

Love

here were slaves in those days, slaves. Not just the white masters who owned slaves in the Americas. No, slaves – of love. When women didn't know why they were with the man, except that they needed the financial support, or the political support, to even be on this planet – yeah, they were slaves all right."

Nora's grandma was speaking that day in May, that very important day, as they sat together in the younger woman's bedroom. Granny continued, "Yes, you see my child, the women I knew couldn't make it on their own."

"Why not?" And why did Granny have to be running off at the mouth about this right now? There were too many things to do. But she respected Gran, so she did her best to tolerate the strange words of this 89 year-old woman, the feisty one, the one the rest of the family, even her own mother, once said, "Your grandma's a bit over the edge, so don't bother listening to half of what she says."

But, although fidgety and uptight, Nora kept tuning in to this dear person. After all, she was the one who had taken her in after her mother died of a heart attack. Nora was just 16, and it was a terrible loss to a sensitive girl at that age, one with no sense of direction in her life. And yes, she'd made some serious mistakes in her life. But Granny had always been there for her.

Now, at 40, Nora was fanning herself with a white lacy handkerchief and lifting up her arms, trying to block nervous perspiration from flowing down her sides and wetting her dress.

Granny continued, "Oh, you think you can earn a living and live the rest of your life without a commitment to a man?"

"No, Gran, this isn't what I meant at all. Besides, I *have* been earning a pretty good wage with my sales position, you know that."

"I know you have, Darlin', I just meant without a commitment to a man."

"Gran, I *was* committed to Billy, remember? But that sure didn't work out."

"I know I know, I watched you get in over your head and I just couldn't talk you out of it. I think you wanted a father and he wanted a mama... you were both too young. Nineteen is just too young."

"But I stuck it out for 7 years, didn't I? Even when Billy never came home some nights and he was drinking heavily and I just never knew where he was."

The old woman patted Nora's hand. Then she got up stiffly from the bed and rubbed the side of her leg and grimaced. "Ooooh, this damned sciatica. What a day to have it act up like this."

"Can I do something Gran? Want an aspirin?"

"You've got enough to think about, Hon. No, I'll just keep moving around here; that always helps. I just can't stay still for too long or I seize up." She smiled through her gritted teeth. "Hey, maybe that could be a motto for life, eh? Keep moving, else you'll be sorry."

They both chuckled. Nora walked gingerly over to the window and pushed it open. She loved this room and how those old windows were surrounded by hemlock trees, and at nights, when she wasn't feeling too sure of herself, when the branches moved, she felt as if they were sweeping her fears and doubts away.

Gran inhaled the fresh spring air and now she was able to take stronger steps back and forth at the end of the bed. Revitalized, her voice sounded stronger too: "Well, I just meant that these days, some women, well... some women are even having children out of wedlock."

"Gran, not now..."

"Why, look at that Angelina Jolie and Brad Pitt. I read that they have six children and they're not even married."

"That's their business, isn't it, Gran? Besides, I think they're good parents and their kids seem happy."

"Well, in my day, well that was 80 years ago as I said, these women were sometimes thought of as slaves to their men. But I couldn't stand that."

"So, what did you do then?"

"Well, my dear, I chose to marry a man I didn't love. At least he couldn't enslave my emotions. No, I thought I could hold out and be my own person that way."

You mean you were married to somebody else before Grandpa?

"I never said that."

"Well, what then? I don't understand. I mean, you and Grandpa always seemed close and very happy."

"I never said we weren't. Your Grandpa Tom was quite a fella though. He just waited for me – he wooed me and bided his time. And before you knew it, I was enjoying him more'n I ever thought I would. I grew to love him."

"Yeah?"

"Yes. I guess that's why we had six children – and your Mama was so beloved. She was our baby." Granny's voice dropped and her eyes shone with old tears.

Nora smiled though her eyes were stinging too, especially when she reached over to her bureau and picked up the photo of her mother in the silver frame; wishing she could have been here today. "I remember her telling me that a long time ago… that you always pampered her, and called her *your baby* well into her life."

"That's true... But you know, Sugar, don't think you have to figure it all out."

"Oh, Gran, I can hardly figure anything at all out... I thought I loved Billy 20 years ago, and that sure didn't work out."

"No, but I think you learned from it, don't you?"

"I sure hope so. But it was hard on both of us... I hope he's okay, whatever he's doing."

Granny nodded. "Yes, he wasn't a bad kid – just mixed up, that's for sure."

"I'd sure like to figure out love, though. I thought I loved Mark and then he had to go and make me so mad last night – being out so late with the boys, not answering the phone. Making me furious when I asked him to do something special today, but he said he had something special to do too... and he sounded tense and short with me. So, feeling like I did, I wondered if I should even go through with it. I really wasn't sure how I felt! I mean... is that love?" Her voice quavered. She brushed the dark hair out of her eyes and looked away, not wanting the older woman to see her tears welling up – forgetting how well Gran knew her.

"Love? You've gotta be in *like* first – then the rest will just fall into place. You'll see." Gran reached out and took her face in her hands, so Nora was compelled to gaze into those loving green eyes – of the one person in her life she had always trusted.

"You really think so, Gran?"

"I know so. Now, go get yourself ready – and we'll get on with this wedding, okay?"

Nora felt a smile creep across her mouth, and in spite of everything she had been feeling that day, in spite of her anger and upset at this man waiting downstairs, she nodded. She recalled the little things he did for her, the way his gaze stayed right on her as she recounted a challenging day at work, or when she told him the sad times from her younger years, or how he puffed up proudly when he introduced her to his friends, or how he just held her hand and didn't say much when she simply wanted quiet that evening, or how she could ask him anything and he most always came through. He was a good man. Yeah, she knew one thing; she was at least *in like* with Mark – so she could commit to that.

And she'd never have to be his slave.

Rainbow Riding

I was on duty that night at the forty-second precinct when that woman came in, and I had to book her again: "State your name."

"Blanche Rider, but I'm gonna change that soon."

"That'll do for now. State your age."

"Well, I seldom mention it, officer, I mean, what's the point of that?"

"State your age I said."

"If you insist… Fifty-three."

"Don't you think you're a bit old for this?"

"A person's never too old for anything, I'm sure of that."

"Well, this thing you say you've been doing is crazy. I mean, I've heard of bungee jumping and hang gliding, but what you've been doing is sheer nuts."

"Oh no, it's exhilarating! Everybody should do it."

"So, what did you say it was again? I mean, it sounds so crazy that nobody can fathom a person... riding up in the sky, flying... sounds like a *trip* to me."

"It's called Rainbow Riding."

"That's what I thought you said. Least, that's what the Captain put down on your file last time. *Rainbow Riding.*"

"Oh yes, it's wonderful. Would you like me to explain it?"

"Never mind lady, you're gonna spend some time in the clink tonight, and when you come down from whatever you're on then you can give it to me in detail."

So, Blanche went into the cell that night.

I was sitting next to that big cell, and she was spinning her yarn to several of the women in there, I overheard some of it. And as I had nothing much to do that night except a bit of paper-work, I tuned in. Sure was better than Reality TV. Crazy.

Anyway, in that drunk tank – that's what we called it – there were some ladies of the night, one or two who'd had too much to drink, and a real mix of others: a couple who got into fights, one woman whose pimp had beaten her up and she'd called the police. Bessie, a regular visitor there, and ol' Franny, whose pimp got to her bad.

Now, strange though this sounds, when those dames were released in the morning, some of them actually *looked* different. And a couple of them said that they were transformed. Even Bessie said she was coming clean, wasn't gonna go down on the streets again… she just knew there was another way to live. And ol' Franny, well, she said she planned to change her very life. I tell you, my eyes began to bug out of my head. But I guess it wasn't so surprising from what I heard this Blanche woman talking about most of the night.

Even Chelsea Harris, who was in there for boozing it up, well she looked changed too. She told me this: "Blanche could be a teacher to the kids I work with at Covenant House. I tell all those kids that I want them to break free of anything that's holding them back. For sure, they need to listen to Blanche."

"Why? What's so special about this dame?" I asked her. But I think I already knew – from listening in to that "reality show" in the cell. Matter of fact, I'd watched those girls gather around Blanche as she sat there in the corner – it was like watching little kids sitting around a fire with an Elder."

"Well, wait till I tell you what she told us. Blanche said..."

"I was out riding my motorcycle late that Friday, feeling down, feeling bad about life, and so I rode by the river. And before I knew it, thunder began to roll and lightning flashed, way out there, miles away. Then, it cleared. And suddenly, there was a beautiful rainbow – huge! A magnificent arc curved over my head. So, I rode right to the tip of it, you know, where the pot of gold might be. Then, an amazing thing happened... She smiled such a beatific grin and it spread all over her face and I swear she looked like an angel at that moment.

"Here she was, 53 years old (I'd heard her telling you that when you checked her in), not that attractive, not very tall, a little bit overweight, long mousy brown hair down her back, and standing there in her leather motorcycle jacket and chaps; she wouldn't have stood out in a crowd for beauty, if you know what I mean. But right then, she was shining like a holy star in the east. I tell you, it was a miracle right in front of my very eyes."

Being the nuisance cop I am, I egged her on. I knew some of what she was going to tell me, but I guess I needed to hear it again. I mean, desk duty can get a bit boring. "So, what did she say?"

"Okay, then Blanche said some things that if you hadn't been there, you'd think she was making it up. But I believed her. It was the way she was saying it, like, you know, with passion in her voice. And her eyes were shining bright... I tell you, she darned near had a halo around her head. I'm kidding you not."

"What else did Blanche say?" On my beat I'd seen Chelsea around; knew that she worked with kids on the street, but I'd never seen anybody so exuberant about anybody they'd met in jail. I mean, we were used to the mean streets of this city, not gurus for god's sake!

Chelsea's eyes were really sparkling now, as if she'd met Jesus Christ himself. "Okay," she quipped, this is what Blanche told us..."

"When I got to the end of that rainbow, I honestly looked for a pot of gold. But it wasn't there. However, there was something else. The ends of that rainbow were like ribbons of road, all colored and beautiful, just beckoning me to cycle on. So, I did.

"I chose that shining yellow ribbon road, and when I eased my ol' hog Harley onto it, slowly at first, well you know, I suddenly felt much happier – as if a huge weight had lifted. My depression was gone. So, I rode on that yellow road for awhile, until it began to rise higher and higher, until I glanced down and suddenly I was on the orange ribbon. And here, a sense of calmness washed over me, and yet I felt a great sense of zest too. I kept on riding higher and higher..."

"What came next?" I asked. It was fun watching Chelsea tell this story – even though I'd heard most of it.

"Well, then Blanche said, 'I had a surge of power and I found myself on the red ribbon road. It was fast – and hot. So, I zoomed up that strip as if it were a power spot in the sky. Actually, it took me in a way where I found myself remembering my dreams – and believing I could actually do them! Amazing. I remembered things I'd always wanted to do – like dance in front of huge audiences, and paint huge canvases, and make movies that will touch people's hearts, and write songs...'"

"Yeah, Blanche's face was glowing now and she looked about 16 years old."

"Up and up I went, higher and higher," she said, "to the peak. To where I knew I wasn't alone anymore. Up into the purple ribbon, where I felt a sense of opening into vastness, where I'd never gone before. It was like my whole life stretched out in front of me and it didn't matter where I was headed – only that I would enjoy the ride; that *all* was well – right where I was at that moment. At that peak, everything was glistening silver, all the colors melted into one another, and I was just carried high above this world. Into what I think heaven must be. Into that place where time stops."

"Did Blanche say she was scared?" I asked her.

"She said, 'Oh no, there was no fear. Something else came… When I pointed my cycle into the green then, I felt my whole chest open up, like my heart was expanding. I roared up that green road and it seemed to envelop me in its tendrils and say, *There, there now… all is well… relax. Just let yourself go.* And so I did.

"Then, I was on the blue ribbon and once again, the indigo, then I felt myself coming down from the peak, and into all the colors together; calmer and more peaceful than I'd ever been. Trusting that if a rainbow could hold me in its arms, wrap all those tendril color roads around me, that I'd never doubt myself again."

"So, she must've had a conniption being locked up in that cell last night then, huh?"

"No, Blanche said, that it doesn't matter what happens to her in this world, she can see above it; that her heart is open to trust, that all a person has to do is ask for what she wants, and it's there, right before you."

"She said, 'I heard that voice loud and clear while I was zooming up on top of that rainbow. Ask and ye shall receive. And then, I heard, *'Demand that the truth of yourself be seen again, and be willing to see your own magnificence.'*

"So, I asked her if she could see it now. I really wanted to know... And this is what Blanche said..."

"When I came down from that motorcycle ride into heaven, I was different. Could never go back to the way I was."

"What did she mean?" Here I was, the stern cop getting into this crazy story. But I wanted to know more.

"Well, I not only demand truth from myself and everybody else, but I can now see people's magnificence. And when I see it in them, I am beginning to believe it in myself. We are mirrors, that's the truth. We're all mirrors of each other. So, if I see beauty in you, I get to see it in myself. Simple, huh?"

Chelsea added, "Course, I said, 'It might be simple, but I don't think it's so easy. What if you see something negative in the other person? Is that a mirror for you too?'"

"Blanche said, 'Yep. But that's how I learn.'"

Oh jeez, the old cop of myself pondered this hard. I mean, I'm a pragmatic, no-nonsense guy and I don't want no guff from anybody. But I had to think on it. My next door neighbor was bugging me and I didn't really want to think that he was a *mirror* of me. But when I thought about that young paper boy who was very kind to me, and always smiled every time I bought a paper from him – and asked if there was anything he could do for me – well, I liked that thought.

I was sorta in my reverie for awhile, but suddenly Blanche returned from the washroom, primping at her long hair, with bright red lipstick on her mouth. Yeah, there she was, right in front of me, but speaking to Chelsea: "Hey, listen, I think there's thunder in them thar hills. Come on, let's go. Maybe we'll get to ride another rainbow."

I watched the two of them walk out of the station together, wondering what was next.

One month later, I was at my desk in the Police Department when a Fax came in, MISSING PERSON

REPORT. *Chelsea Harris has not been seen for over a month now. Anyone knowing of her whereabouts please report that information.*

I shook my head, reached for my cigs, lit up and inhaled deeply. Nobody would ever believe me if I told them she was probably Rainbow Riding up in heaven. I shook my head and smiled. I'm sure she was having a great time wherever she was, so why bring her back down to earth?

A New Canvas

*W*hat the hell's it all about anyway? You call yourself an artist? You haven't painted one thing in over two weeks and that one canvas of the beautiful Iris in full bloom looks totally wilted. Ah, who gives a damn anyway? Nobody's ever going to see anything I paint. You probably won't even last 'til then, ol' girl.

What's the point of staying around anyway? Hand's too heavy to pick up a brush, heart's too dense to see an iris, eyes too squinty to get it all right anymore. I'm tired. Called Lori today and she hasn't even returned my call. You'd think a daughter might care. No, too busy for that. Too busy for love. Ha... I know that one. Now, I can't even remember what all the fuss and bother was for.

Charlotte Wheaton lay listlessly on her bed glancing out the window as the sunlight played on her belly, warming her legs, and her groin too; just the way one of her lovers used to. Harvis was especially nice, so loving. She ran her own hand across the warmth of her belly and then left it there for awhile. Glancing down at it, she studied the heavy ring on her long slender finger, her middle one; it was the ring he gave her when they'd had that mini-marriage.

Neither one wanted the whole legal thing, but that ceremony was as close and courageous as either could muster. They'd stood together in the broad light of day, naked and proud, opening up as much as they could to each other and the sight of God *up thar in the heavens* as Harvis had put it with that slow Texan drawl. The only thing he'd wanted to wear was his shoes because his feet hurt without the arch supports. So she'd kept her sandals on too –and draped a silk scarf ceremoniously around her soft dark curly hair to frame her face, *like a Madonna* – that's what Harvis said that day. Together, they pledged their troth: to be as loving as they possibly could, and tell each other the truth always. Well, the truth nearly did them in…

When she'd confided to him about Glenn, oh that was bad… While Harvis was away on that long trip to Italy, and she couldn't go because of the art show she was working on, Glenn had helped her with the framing and he'd been so attentive. Well, hearing about that, Harvis had gone ballistic, and he'd nearly shot the man!

Hey, what was truth all about if you couldn't even say what was real? It wasn't that Glenn was any more a man than Harvis – but he was *there*, and "hubby" wasn't. Now, Harvis wasn't there at all anymore –couldn't take the pressure of any other men around.

He wanted to own her, possess her soul, make her his own. But how could she be his when she wasn't even her own self? How could she let him take her soul when she hadn't even found it?

The union didn't last more than a year. But it had been quite wonderful there for that time. She did love him – and still wore his ring. As she glanced at that large silver men's design with turquoise and some Navajo symbols on it, she smiled and her thighs tingled.

They'd been crazy-wild together. Passionate. Make love all night and still be able to do their work the next day. He sure made her feel like a woman desired. Her right hand stroked her breasts, her left hand stayed closer to her groin.

"Damn, I'm even too tired for that," she muttered out loud. "Who would've ever thought it? Me, *proverbial love goddess*." Yeah, that's what Jose had said when she'd lain with him – and they'd flown to South America and he introduced her to his Mamacita and was prepared to leave his whole family for her. Never had he been so smitten. Never had he loved as he did Charlotte.

But Mama and the little sibling bambinos were too much for Jose, and his Catholic conscience got the better of him. Alas, he wrote her that his Papa had died and Mamma needed him and well, he couldn't leave just yet and would she wait...

Sure. For about a week or two she'd waited. But her body wouldn't let her wait too long. When her show was at the Vancouver Museum and Walter praised her art and her color and her passion, she let him keep on raving about her – and when he drove her home and wanted to come in, she let him... and... he was sweet. Even though he was bi-sexual and hadn't really been with a woman for some time, she believed she could make him forget men – for awhile anyway. Besides, his boyfriend was away and, well, it had just happened. Only once or twice. And she always made him wear a condom – which back then was quite avant guard – 'cause she just didn't fancy his being with some fellow – and then her. Anyway, he was wonderful and once again she'd known her powers of seduction.

Yes, Walter described her as the *just like the Botticelli* – and she felt that beautiful. She'd heard it all before, but it never hurt to hear it again. Besides, she craved it; had to have that nourishment. After that, she would bounce out of bed and splash bright and happy colors onto her canvas. And it would sell!

Charlotte stumbled into the bathroom and then grabbed her white terry cloth robe on the back of the door. The mirrors were too revealing. When did she get that pot belly? And saggy breasts? Who was that stranger in that looking glass? Her hair was still long and thick, but now the dark brown was streaked with so much gray. Her once strong mouth was saggy at the edges and her eyes that used to open wide were now heavy lidded with dark circles ringing them –like a luminescent bird at the edge of a dark puddle. Everything was just a bit darker, as if in the shadows of time, the shadows of her own life.

Nobody ever talked about this time.

Besides, she never even thought she'd live into her fifties; always believed she'd probably check out early. Like her father. But she'd thrown out all pills and razor blades just in case she'd had the urge to do it before she was good and ready. Glancing in the medicine cabinet, rifling through the bottles, my god, how had she missed this one? It was old; probably didn't have any effect anymore; expiration date was long overdue. Maybe it would still do the trick. But what if it only made her sleep for two days and then somebody found her in that state? Besides, Judy was coming in tomorrow wasn't she? Damn it, why had she hired her to clean up anyway?

What difference did it make if her place was tidy or not? In the old days she could live with mess in her studio, and be in such a creative frenzy she never noticed. All she ever did was paint and make love and paint some more and eat a little and then make love.

There was always some man who loved her. Always some man...

But there hadn't been one for over five years now. Was there something wrong with her? Was she that undesirable? *Invisible* was more like it. She could walk down Robson Street and nobody would even notice her. Oh, once in a while she'd bump into a friend of course. But no man saw her. No man met her eyes. Not even when she stared right at one.

Now, she'd given up looking.

She wandered into her studio, bare-footed, tousled from lying in bed most of the day. She stared at her canvases, warily, as if they were strangers now, strangers who had some kind of power over her. These canvases, once her friends, once her beloveds... Her chest ached – so fiercely she was brought to her knees, then down fully onto the linoleum where, inadvertently, she curled up on that cold floor. And all the heaviness in her emptied out – as if all the old hard dried oil paint, once squirted lovingly and passionately onto a canvas, now melted and slid off – like the blood of her last, and final, period. There, curled into the fetal shape of a newborn, her bare-feet drawn up to her chest, she sobbed and convulsed – and finally pushed out of that fiftyish cocoon she'd been trapped in, for too long.

Slowly, oh so slowly, after this tempestuous labor, she rolled onto her back and lay there. All of her senses pulsing wide open.

As her head rolled to her right, she gazed at one painting over there in the corner. She hadn't even noticed it before. There it was: A child; eyes risen up to the sky, blue background, a sprig of weeds in the child's hand.

Painfully, rubbing her lower back, she stood up on shaky legs, and stared at that painting – as if it were an apparition. Her legs moved and she took three steps over to it. How did it get here? Oh, god, her mother... after her mother died last year the executors must have sent it. My god, mother, did you do that?

No, I did. It was me.

She pulled the canvas from its hiding place and placed it on the easel. The child stared back at her: Wide eyed. Waiting...

But it wasn't finished. The mouth wasn't right. It was too sad. Surely, no child should look so lonely. Oh child, I shall complete you. Oh God, I must. I can't do one ruddy thing until I get you right. I see you my baby. Oh darling, yes, I remember you. I shall bring you back to life!

Charlotte reached for her paints and palette; squirted color onto it; turquoise, *let the sky be even more brilliant, and yellow for her hair – let her glow in the sunshine.* As she picked up her favorite brush, she whispered, Yes, this child needs me!

Why Stay?

*W*hy do I have to stay here in this place when I feel like running away? Sure, I have a beautiful home, two great kids, lots of income from my online business, even an office to call my own – so why am I so mad?

Last night, I had three of my old college buddies over for dinner and we had a great time together. But maybe I was jealous – a bit, anyway. I mean, Marci talked about her job that takes her to France every month, to Paris – and she has a lover there – and one here too. She says she's opening up. Yeah, I guess! "Jean Louis is such a passionate lover, even loves to kiss me all over." Right. Who wouldn't love that?

Sandra, well, she's pretty happy too, or seems to be. Married Doug, her college sweetheart and they're still together. Only one problem – Doug might be gay. "Well, it doesn't really bother me too much... I mean, he is such a good provider." Yikes! I couldn't live with that.

Georgi: She looks beautiful, might have had a few tucks and Botox treatments but she's doing okay. Does ramp modeling in New York, and then flies off to Cannes and hobnobs with the likes of George Cluny and his latest girlfriend. But is she happy? Really?

How do I compare myself? And why am I feeling so mad? Hey, Roberta Jane Johnson, you think that at age 49 you're doing so bad?

Look at this home you live in. And your children. Sure, they're not perfect, but they certainly are high functioning; they love their sports and they're loving kids. Nine and 15, ages that still need their mother. So look, I should *not* be flying off to Paris or L.A. or New York. And would I want a gay husband, who's been with some man before coming home to me?

Okay, Paul is not very charismatic, not the one people listen to while we have dinner parties – sometimes he hardly gets a word in. But he's steady. He's a good lover. And he comes home every night. Hey girl, you're not doing so bad I'd say.

So get off your *mad*. You're just cranky 'cause there's still a lot to clean up from last night's party. But Donnie and Jamie will be home soon. Put a smile on, Robbie. Life is much better than you ever thought it would be. And for sure, I am opening up even more to who I really am.

Still Here

*W*ho woulda thought I'd be the one still left here? Still sitting on this ol' porch, still rocking my chair, the one my hubbie painted my favorite color, periwinkle blue. Oh, he'd laugh at that silly name for a color and say, 'Peri, that man in the moon must be winkin' at us, eh?' Then, he'd add with a little grin and that wicked smile of his, 'He cain't winkle his little winki – but I can still do it.'

"Oh, Chester, I'd say, and we'd both crack up."

Kelly Bowen kept writing in her notepad; she had an assignment so she was sticking it out. Besides, what would this old lady say next?

Marjorie, 95 years old, kept on going, as if she hadn't noticed the embarrassment of this young 19-year-old. After all, *she* was the one who came knocking on her door to ask if she could interview her, so hell, she was going to say whatever came into her mind.

"Then, as if my darlin' Chester just remembered something, he'd stop rockin' his sturdy ol' brown chair, his brows would furrow like a bear trying to open a can of peaches, and he'd reach for the amber drink at the side table. *Coca Cola* he always said, but we both knew it was laced good with rum. Benjamin, our son brought it back a few years ago from Jamaica: *'to heal the pain of retirement,'* he said to his Dad. But it never did; only made him mean and cranky. Why, any time Chester would try to take the wrinkle outa his winki, well, he'd finally roll off me with such a disgusted look, and pretend it didn't matter.

"Course it mattered. Well, it used to: back in the old days, no, really the new days. That man kept me happy and smiling, for sure. We'd make love then laugh and have a cig and make love again, till we was sweating and the sheets soakin' wet… Oh, I shouldn't be telling you all this…"

Kelly's face was beet red, but she continued to write; grinned slightly and nodded to the old woman in the blue chair, "It's okay."

Marjorie rambled on, "Well, in the mornings he'd be up early, and I'd hear him whistling as he shaved. Then he'd come and kiss me on the cheek and tell me to stay put, that he could get his own breakfast 'cause I wasn't too well, really, I mean I wasn't sure why, but I guess the arthritis was creeping into my body. Well, then I'd smell the coffee and soon, I'd hear his ol' Pontiac rev up – then, I wouldn't see him till supper time... You sure you want me to talk like this?"

"Marjorie, I mean Mrs. Springer, I already said that I want to learn your story so I can write it up. So, if you don't talk, I won't have anything to put on the page. My editor is insisting I get this story in soon because I'm writing about older people and I want to know how you've been aging so well."

"Okay then, Kelly, I'll keep going if you don't mind. It helps to clear the cobwebs in my mind. Ninety-five's getting up there now, ain't it?

"Oh, look at that sunset tonight. The lilac bushes are sure smelling sweet now after the rain this morning. But my heart hurts when I talk about him this way 'cause it feels like he isn't even gone, you know? Anyway, it was mighty fine of you to come by and bring me this soup. Delicious."

"Thanks," murmured Kelly, and smiled at her.

Marjorie slurped her vegetable soup and smacked on her piece of toast slathered with strawberry jam. "Maybe he really isn't gone."

Kelly frowned. Then, she scribbled something in her notebook. "What do you mean?"

The old lady didn't answer, just gazed out to the trees for a few minutes. Finally, she said, "Don't worry 'bout cleaning up the dishes in there 'cause Bertha's supposed to come by tomorrow morning and give me a bath."

"Well, that's nice, isn't it?"

"You might say so… you who are so young. But damn it anyway, I used to love my own baths, I'd lie there in bubbles up to my armpits and it was luxury I'll tell you. Didn't happen often, but Chester keeps on saying that it'll make me better, so he buys these bath salts and I pour them in…

"You mean he *used* to do that…"

Marjorie coughed on a piece of toast, then inhaled deeply. "Sometimes, he used to climb in there with me if he came home early – 'specially when he'd had a hard day…

I can always tell by the look on his face... I mean, *could*. Besides, he always had to have his beer, and by then he'd stink of it. You can always tell how many by the smell on his breath."

Kelly cleared her throat. "Mrs. Springer, how long has it been since he passed on?"

"Who said he did? You don't know everything now do you? You're so young. You don't know that he's still here... in his own way... sometimes as clear as day."

"Did he talk to you about his work, then?"

"Not always. But if it was a good selling day he'd brag about how many vacuum cleaners he'd sold, and his chest would puff up. But other days, oooh, ooh, the air was black and sparking red cinders of his rage and you didn't want to go near him... But I don't focus on those times."

The young woman gazed directly into Marjorie's eyes now and Kelly's eyes were like a cocker spaniel's; you could have told her anything and you'd feel that she still cared for you.

Marjorie must have been reminded of the pet she once had, and so she felt comfortable looking into the young woman's cocker spaniel eyes. "We had one of those dogs for a long time but he was hit by a car – and after that, Chester chose other breeds, like German Shepherds, or Border Collies 'cause he thought they was a lot smarter than the little blond doggie; that one just never listened."

"You said that you didn't like thinking about some of the challenging times, so what do you focus on?"

"I try to remember the little things, like his hands with the beautiful straight nails, and his palms, so soft. Or the way his teeth were so straight, except for the one eye tooth that kinda stuck out a bit, but I liked it. Or his beard. At first, it was half-way down his chest when we met, but then gradually, he trimmed it. Besides, when our first son was born, he'd pull it. So, he finally trimmed it close to his chin, and I liked that a lot better." She giggled out loud.

Kelly chuckled too. "What else?"

"I liked it that even when he was scolding the boys, his voice was still soft, and he'd take them onto his lap and at the same minute he was admonishing them, he'd still be loving them.

"Yeah, I never knew I'd be without him. I mean I'm the one who hasn't been well all these years... Arthritis takes its toll... So how could he go before me?"

"It must have been so hard on you. I'm sorry for your loss..."

Marjorie's eyes blinked hard, and she shook her head as if in confusion. Then, her eyes filled with tears as she gazed right at Kelly, as if she was looking right through her. "Look, girlie, didn't I tell you that he really isn't gone? Can't you feel him here? He's in that breeze across your face. He's in the soup I just ate. He's sitting right there next to you in his brown chair. Sometimes Chester sits in that old Pontiac out there. He's here I tell you..."

Kelly raised her overweight body slowly from her red chair, the one next to Chester's brown one. Then she slowly walked into the kitchen and dialed her phone. Her boss at the magazine had told her there'd be days like this. Who to believe? What difference did it make whether the old lady still thought her husband was here or not? But would she be all right if she kept on living in the past? Was this dementia? Would she still think that he'd be coming home to have a bath with her? Who would look after her? Shouldn't she call the authorities?

The line was busy at her office. So, she turned off the pot of soup on the stove, sighed heavily, closed her eyes for a moment and just stood there quietly. Feeling more centered, she ambled out to the porch again. The old lady was slumped in her chair.

Kelly gazed out to the lilac bush, the one near the driveway, where the old Pontiac was parked. Just for a moment, she thought she saw the lights of the old car flicker.

Marjorie sighed deeply, and her smile seemed to spread all over her face. Then she went still. Too still.

Kelly perched there on that old rickety porch, her eyes wide, scratching her head. Maybe this was the best way to age. And the best way to go. Whose reality was better, really?

Who Was She Anyway?

any whispered that she was an untamed dilettante, dancing naked in the moonlight, doing whatever she was driven to do, without concern for the outcome. But Claire would always say that something would come out from her actions. She'd been practicing avoidance for forty years, and people often perceived her as stuck-up, aloof, or flighty; a person with no grounding, no particular part of the earth to stand upon. Others saw her as a smart business woman, self-made; a mover and a shaker, somebody who shakes up the status quo.

Little did they know the truth.

She was good at her act: because she did not want anyone to know who she was. Why? Because if they knew, she'd lose her anonymity. If they knew, she wouldn't have

74

her sacred time alone. She could pretend she wasn't home when she chose not to answer the phone. She could hide out, and delight in their guesses as to where she'd gone for that week. She could pretend she had flown off to England. Or Nepal. Or Timbuktu. This was her time to be solitary.

What did she really do?

She'd cross off whole sections of her day-timer. Then, she'd venture out in the middle of the night, from her well-heeled condo in Santa Monica, climb into her old Jag XKE, and drive way, way up the Pacific Coast Highway – to Zuma Beach. This is where the waves pummeled their full round white-spraying bodies into the sand – where the sea air was clean and those wild surfer waves stirred her senses awake and reminded her that places on this planet were still wild and pristine.

She'd wrap her orange shawl around her body – it matched her hair – then pad along the ragged shoreline in her bare feet. After a long trek, her orange locks blowing wild around her face, she would pick up a few pebbles and place them in a circle further up on the sand. As she tiptoed into this sacred space, she would inhale deeply several times, do a moon salutation – and call upon the spirits of all who had gone before her: Mom, Dad, brother John, her old granny, and, most of all, her dearest love, Clive. In that little space she would gaze into the millions of stars in that black sky, then slowly, focus upon the brightest star– and commune with those beloveds who were now, most probably, on Pleiades.

For hours she'd sit there. Cold, shivering, she'd wrap her shawl more tightly, and do her best to ignore any discomfort; just rise above her body; after all, this was her sacred time.

When the sky began to lighten, she'd stand up, raise her hands in prayer position and bow to the sky.

Later, she would stumble stiff-legged to her car, rubbing her back as she flopped onto the soft leather seat covers and gently clicked the car door after her. Her face felt radiant and she'd smile in that soft familiar way, where she knew her soul was singing.

She was alive!

Nobody knew who she really was. But she knew. And that was enough.

Monday Morning

*I*t's raining in big huge globs onto the window as she pulls up her knees to rest her book there, so as not to waken him – nor see him leave. Last night was magical, in ways no one else would ever believe. But it happened, and no one could take *that* away from her. He was really here...

His lithe, brown-skinned hard body lay softly breathing, six inches from her, his black hair tufted up on her pillow; the one she never used except to balance the look of her bed, or to toss her leg over it pretending it was a living body. Now, even in sleep, he made her tremble involuntarily, and she raised her left hand to her mouth and stuck her thumb in, nibbling on the cuticle. With her other hand, she raised her pen to the page and began to write.

Okay, Marianna, what now? There's this amazing man in your bed and you only met him yesterday. Do they call this a one-night stand? Well, it's only been one night, but who's to say it won't be more than that? At this ripe old-age of 43, I'd say it's time...

The pen stopped moving and she put her red journal down, gazing over to him again. His hand was draped across his mid-section and she studied the lean lines, the straight cut short nails, the long fingers; those of an artist or someone who should use those hands artistically – to mold soft wet clay, to cup it as he had done with her breasts last night. On this wet Monday morning, she remembered the molding, the cupping, the gentle pressure against the sides of her breasts – so gentle; not hard like Richard had been.

But that was long ago, too long, and she didn't want to remember that now. Not now when she needed new memories.

No, Tomas had pressed lightly, as if he were molding clay, as if each breast truly mattered to him and he wanted to investigate each one and gaze upon them – decide how he would form them in his wet clay. Each one, he had touched in this way, and then he'd stroked and pressed every tiny inch of her upper chest, as if he'd never known such a body. As if hers was special, as if her flesh was *not* too thick on her bones, as if when he kneaded it, she was his moist clay and he was creating her in the way he wanted. And only then did he move on and explore more of her – with his fingertips, then his palms, and then his lips and his tongue. Oh God, she felt the heat rise in her now, coming from in-between her breasts and up past her neck, until her face was flaming. And she was smiling; down further, her vagina was wet again.

Could she waken him?

But he would leave.

On Monday mornings, the world went back to normal, slipped into that righted place, as if the dolls had not leapt off their shelves and danced all night; as if the calliope had not played and the crowd cheered; as if the phoenix had not flown up from the sidelines, flown up with wings spread wide, flown up to the moon. Was that possible?

Through the dreary gray outside, now the raindrops looked like little crystals there on the window. Beyond them, she noticed the wind chime her daughter had given her, dangling in the frigid air like worn out fingers – and even the old rose bush branch, still green in Vancouver's November, was slightly waving; and the folded summer's red and white umbrella was gyrating rhythmically, like a flag. She'd needed to keep it there when the hot pink and purple petunias died, to remind herself of color. God, November was so dreary.

She hadn't even written much since Jessica went off to college. She glanced at her photo on the green bureau, there beyond the end of her bed; the king-sized, too big for one. She'd thought of selling it after the marriage broke up – but never had. Besides, Richard was seldom home so she'd often slept in it alone. She was so gullible! She believed him that he'd had these late-night clients – that his PR position took him away. Believed him too when he'd said she was getting fat. He'd made her get up on the bed to look at the extra crease of flesh on her thigh – believed him that he wasn't attracted to her like he'd once been. That no man would be...

So, she would come home after her accounting work, dine alone, then eat a few too many chocolate chip cookies as she tried to focus on her writing. She knew she had at least one book in her. But the TV often won out, and besides, it was company – for three years it had been like that... Until last night.

Yesterday, late in the day, she'd gone for a walk along Kits Beach, and there he was. Walking in the rain too; hands deep in his pockets, black eyes flashing some sort of wildness. But she was drawn to him. It was as if she were looking into a mirror, a kind one. So, they'd ambled up to Yew Street, had a coffee at Starbucks, and talked for a long, long time. Then for some reason, she'd never done this before, ever, since Richard had left – she'd asked him back to her place for dinner.

They'd hardly eaten much – ended up in this king-sized bed. And here, the magic had truly begun. Oh, she closed her eyes and smiled again at the memory of it all.

But it was Monday. Now, he would surely leave...

His head turned. His lips made little smacking sounds. Then, as if he sensed her gaze, his eyes fluttered open, and he stared at her.

Just for an instant, she thought, "He doesn't remember me... Or maybe he doesn't like what he sees."

But in his deep basso voice, he muttered, "What're you doing so wide awake?"

"Nothin.'"

"Anything wrong?"

"No... wondering when you've got to go."

He blinked his eyes into focus, "What time is it?"

"About 8:00."

"You want me to go?"

"If you want to..."

"You want me to go?"

In that instant, all the shyness returned, all her doubts, everything Richard had battered her with for 25 years. Oh, it would be so much easier with no heart. After all, it was just the sex, just the need, just two people falling into bed on a Sunday night. It didn't mean anything... Be sophisticated. Don't care. Don't let on.

She inhaled deeply. Oh, what the hell. *Tell the truth for once here girl.* "No, I don't want you to leave... not really."

"Neither do I." He reached over and drew her into him, and ran his hand along her cheek, tenderly, like he cared.

After awhile, with their legs and arms all intertwined and he was gazing into her eyes, she felt something melting inside her, and she started remembering, way, way back, to when she knew a deeper place. To when she was clear; to when she knew who she was. And when she looked into those now-soft dark eyes, where yesterday they were wild, there was a reassuring sparkle inside them that said to her, *This is okay.*

This time, she let herself believe the truth.

So, this Monday morning she was staying put, right where she was.

Filled With Purple

er legs were still trembling from their encounter this afternoon; she couldn't stop thinking of him. Even as she stepped onto the faded blue-carpeted corridor on the fourth floor trying not to let the familiar scents of this old apartment building bother her – like Mrs. Jensen's cabbage soup, Mr. Spencer's burned pork chops, or the mustiness of the hallway – she imagined her neighbors behind those closed doors, fixated on their TVs, mumbling, never going anywhere. Never going anywhere; that was *her* problem too. Mary Smithers certainly hadn't planned to be living with her mother – not at fifty-one years of age.

Key in lock, she hung up her black rain gear on the old coat tree, thudded her rubber boots onto the black plastic tray near the door – her mother hated it if she traipsed across the turquoise carpet with them on. Then she shook out the rain from her green plaid skirt, adjusted her sensible gray sweater and cardigan, and with an elbow rub to her steamed-up round spectacles, she snapped off her too-tight pearl earrings, pressed her strand of real pearls close to her collar-bone, then ambled down the long hallway into the living room. As she arched her head back and ran her hand through her short gray hair, she muttered under her breath: *Darn it, I can't go out with him.*

Mother was on the couch, as usual. "Well, I wondered if you'd be here on time. Humph." Her voice was pitched high.

"Hello, Mother... I usually am. How was your day?" She smiled at the eighty-seven year old woman who laid on the flowered couch and wondered how anyone so tiny could loom so large in one's life.

"Well, I tell you... those people upstairs were making such a racket this afternoon, I could hardly have my nap. The worst thing they ever did was to let children into this building. Why thirty years ago it was a lovely place ... now, they're letting the riff raff in and..."

"Hmm," Mary nodded, feigned interest; then, made a bee-line to the bathroom. But the closed door brought no privacy. The nattering went on and on: when was dinner going to be ready; something about a church bazaar; and, "Did you bring me my special biscuits?"

Mary moaned under her breath and shook her head, "They're on the counter Mother."

She could *nearly* tune out after all these years; nearly. The litany of aches and pains she could shut her ears to, but sometimes it got to her – especially when that acerbic tongue criticized her hair style, mentioned her slight weight-gain, joked at the new lines on her face – that they were just like *hers*.

In the bathroom, she brushed her teeth, inspecting the eye teeth as if for the first time; the passing years changed things; look, now they were turned inward, pushing against the others, crowding them towards her upper lip which was already too pouty from an overbite. Never mind, maybe he hadn't noticed. But she knew she'd smiled at him, must have. Of course he'd noticed! Gordon. Besides, in the past, he never seemed to mind how her teeth looked.

She'd seen him at the store today, at The Bay, where she worked at her new job, the jewelry counter; been there only three weeks; feeling more confident now – till he'd walked right up to her! The gold ring she was placing carefully back in the glass case slid from her grasp and bounced, so she'd had to get down on her hands and knees to retrieve it. He'd helped her look, and chuckled— but her ears were burning and she felt like a furnace was inside her.

Oh, after all these years, there he was... and she was nineteen again and excited about life, grinning and sparkling and forgetting any passage of time. He asked her if she'd like to go for dinner, and of course she wanted to.

But then, she thought, *Oh my gosh, how could I possibly go out for any evening since Mother needs me – even more since she had the stroke last year. Besides, it's been too long since I've been out to dinner with any man, let alone him. How could I face him across a table?* The hair stood up all over her arms and back just thinking about it. *Anyway, what would I wear?*

He said he'd come by about 8:00, and if she could make it, he'd just wait downstairs in the lobby. After all, no point in facing Mother again, not after the things she'd said to him years ago. If Mary couldn't make it, he'd understand. Just like he always did – those deep brown eyes of his engulfing her with compassion, making her want to dive right in to them.

She bustled into the kitchen and swaddled herself with the huge apron her mother had once sewn. Could she ever muster up the courage to do what she really wanted? She dipped two breasts of chicken in milk and bread crumbs, fried them, boiled potatoes and carrots, mashed them, toasted white bread, cut it diagonally – Mother wouldn't eat it if it were cut any other way – and made the tea; Red Rose, had to be that; if they were out of it, Mother just couldn't digest her meal. Why, once she'd had to run across 16th Avenue in the rain to get it. Now, she served her on her green tray at the couch in the living room, so she wouldn't miss Coronation Street, her favorite show.

"Aren't you eating?"

"Ah, later Mom, I'm not hungry. Need to unwind."

"Humph. You young people have strange ideas. You should eat at the same time every night; it's better for your health."

"Right, Mom."

Mary took refuge in the bathroom, preparing to shower. Her plaid skirt and sweater she hung neatly on the hook at the back of the door, but as she unclasped her sensible white bra, and wriggled out of her panty hose and old white cotton panties, she let them drop onto the bath mat. However, in turning on the shower, she was still cautious, had to make sure it wasn't too hot. Once with this weird old shower she'd nearly scalded herself and that scared her half to death; just one more thing she'd done to lose her confidence.

Could she ever trust herself? Timidly, she stepped in, welcoming the hot water as it pelted her shoulders into a softer slope; breathing in deeply, she moaned a little *"ah"* as the water splattered over her upturned face and all down her naked body. She reveled in the relaxation for a few minutes before reaching for the Dove soap in the pink plastic dish; inhaled the scent of it; pleased that it was lasting as long as it had. Yes, at least some things she could look after. Then she smoothed the satin suds over her neck and arms and small breasts – she still liked touching them –like Gordon used to, so many years ago.

Would he ever again? Tonight?

No. She couldn't go! Venture into that again? She shivered. Besides, she couldn't leave Mother; she got lonely after spending her day all by herself. Well, sometimes she had visitors. *No Mary, you can't go.*

He was buying a watch "for my grandson" he'd said. But he looked just the same. Oh, his hair was grayer now, receding, and he had a slight paunch; but there was that same old gentleness in his face, that same old grin with that space between his teeth – where she used to put her own tongue – the same old full lips she'd sucked on; once upon a time.

"Mary!" The call came from far off. Ye gods, she couldn't even *think* these thoughts without her mother interfering; the same old high-pitched grating voice. "Mary, whatever are you doing? The whole place is steaming up. Why, you'll run up the heating bill."

"Be right out, Mother." She wasn't going to let her upset her tonight – whether she went or not. No, just to linger on *him* made her smile. Perhaps she didn't have to go; just remember... His long fingers on her face, moving up her cheeks toward her eyes, forehead, down again, across her lips, so lightly, exploring, as if he were blind, etching her indelibly... gazing into her eyes, and the way he... *Stop it! You're not going. It's too scary. Why get into that all over again when you've been doing so well on your own.*

She lathered her hair and then slathered that soap all over herself once more; over her breasts, her belly, her bottom, the tops of her thighs, opening... But she quickly rinsed off.

Stepping out, she dried herself carefully, even between her toes, rubbed her whole body vigorously, wanting to rub out the dead cells. Yes, she knew about that stuff, had heard Jolanda at the Clinique counter talk about the importance of cell renewal. And so she rubbed and rubbed with that fluffy towel, because tonight she wanted to scrub away all the age in there, all the nights of crying; all those years in-between them, all the despair she knew was locked in there somewhere. Tonight, no matter what, she wanted fresh skin shining.

She pursed her lips and chastised herself, *Oh Mary, it's just dinner…Forget it…Nothing will happen anyway.* She shook her head. *You're not going.*

She toweled her hair dry, wrapped herself in her old white terry cloth robe which she always left on the back of the door, then padded into her bedroom where she stood for a moment in the middle of the room. Breathing hard.

"Mary! I need more hot water for my tea."

Mary looked around at her bedroom, the single four-poster bed which she always made so precisely every morning; the nine-drawer mahogany dresser with the lacy cloth upon it; the silver brush and mirror set she'd had for years; the picture of her mother and father on their wedding day. The photo of herself when she was just five. She had no idea why she kept that picture, but she could look at it, as if she were looking in a mirror. Yes, sad, sloping shoulders, caved in chest upon which she wore a beautiful gold locket – with teeth marks in it; her own. *Why had she bitten into that locket way back then?*

Why was she even here with her mother? Oh, why had she left Gordon anyway?

"Mary! Can't you hear me?" The decibel level was escalating.

"Be right there, Mother."

She reached into her top drawer on the far left side and brought out something still wrapped in red tissue paper. The package was on the bed now, and she sat there staring at it, her hands suddenly sweaty. Timidly, like a shy child given a too-beautiful present with pink bows and expensive paper, she unwrapped it –until its purple satin was exposed. She could smell its newness, hear its suggestive little whispers, nudging her; where? Back to somebody she once knew? Yes, a beautiful purple teddy.

Wiping her hands on the bedspread, she ran her palms over the satin, thrilling at the sleekness of it. Little tremors jerked her arms and chest and she couldn't help smiling; gleefully. With a little yank, she removed the tags, then dropped her robe and held up the slinky thing in front of her naked body.

She put it on.

Oooh, yes, this must have been why she bought this last January. On sale too. And the saleslady had suggested that she complete the outfit with a beautiful purple satin blouse and purple silk panty hose. "You just never know when you'll want this," said the bleached blond gum-chewing clerk. "Why, I always keep this kind of thing in my drawer, if you know what I mean." Then she'd winked at her.

Face flaming, Mary bought the items just to get out of the store. She had never purchased anything so outlandish in her whole life.

But something had nagged at her that day. It was a day when she wondered if she could even live anymore; a day when everything was black and dull and rainy in Vancouver; when the world was wet and heavy and too hard to hold in her empty heart. So she'd left that lingerie store with a $175 purchase on her Master Card – if you can imagine – but she just had to do it. Whether she ever put the things on, they were hers. And they were, somehow, crucial. As she clutched her bag filled with purple and carried it back home on the bus to 16th Avenue, it was for her, a little bag of mystery, of life.

"Mary! Whatever are you doing?" Her mother whined into her reverie.

Mary's voice sounded sharp to her own ears when she answered her. "I said I'd be right there, now please hang on will you?"

From another drawer, she pulled out and put on the purple panty hose. Then from under a gray jacket in her closet, claimed the purple blouse and draped the satin over her shoulders. As she buttoned it across her breasts, encased in the purple body suit, plumped up they were in that purple, she stood there, eyes wide, breathing in and out, in and out, suddenly a bit dizzy. *Calm down, girl, you're not even going, so why be so nervous. You're just trying these things on.*

"Mary, please... I need my tea."

Mary threw her robe over her purple lingerie, and stomped out to serve her mother. Pausing beside her though, she gazed at the little sparrow-like woman on the couch, noticed a few bald spots that used to sprout her thick silver hair. Her once robust size 14 had shrunk to an 8; her great melon breasts were now pitted apricots; her face was hollow. And her once beautiful hands that used to play Chopin's Etudes with such tenderness were knotted in-between dark liver spots with heavily- roped veins.

Fondly, Mary plumped up her pillow. *She might not be around very long.* She winced and rubbed her own chest; then brought her a refill on her tea. But the older woman, lost in her TV program, hardly looked at her; just absently nodded.

Back in her room, robe off again, she shook her head at the purple image in her mirror. *It was all ridiculous.* Dejectedly, she flopped onto her bed and stared at the ceiling.

I'm not going to go. My life is set here. She gave me refuge when I needed it most... when the big job was gone... when I was losing my mind. At least I can look after her now. Who else will? Not sister Joyce, oh no. She defected to Mexico and never even visits—says she's too busy. Right. So, I'm it.

Besides, if your own mother hardly glances at you, isn't it crazy to even think anybody else will? Wasn't that what my shrink tried to teach me? To let go of "magical thinking?" To simply accept reality as it is. I've got a roof over my head, no real cares except having to get myself ready for work every day, and then help out at home with Mother. And I do love her.

True, she'd been trying to get her attention for years, but no matter what she did, she knew her mother wasn't likely to change.

Her eyes stung. Blinking fast, she continued to stare at the yellowed ceiling. Why, after all these years was she here? How *did* she get back here?

She and Gordon were best friends, once, loved each other passionately. With him, she could be silly and funny and talk about art and writing poetry and flying saucers and flying to the moon. But she'd left him – because he was Catholic and Italian and his father was a shoe-repair man, and her father was a furniture merchant – so she knew he would never fit in with her family. And her mother always wanted someone better for her and... oh God, because she was absolutely stupid then...

A few years later, she'd married Ken, a man from a "good family," with possibilities; someone who was on the way up – and suddenly, *she* was on the way down. He'd walked out on her, just after she'd given birth to Tommy. So how could he have known that Tommy wouldn't be healthy, that he would die 12 years later, that she would have a nervous breakdown over the anguish of it. With very little money, she couldn't have survived unless her mother had offered her this place to live – rent free.

But nothing was free. She was finding that out.

Teeth pressed tight to her bottom lip, she sat up and slowly undid the buttons on the purple blouse. Removing it, she wandered to the closet, and suddenly noticed her old standby; her long black skirt, tulip shaped with the little flare just at the bottom. And there, underneath it, the black cowboy boots that Joyce had once given her.

Rolling her eyes at herself as if her younger sibling were right there in the room with her, she pulled on those boots. Put on the skirt, and re-buttoned the blouse. And there, in the mirror at the back of her door, she looked hard. Yes, her hair was unkempt and there wasn't one trace of makeup on that shiny face. But staring back with very wide eyes was a fresh-faced woman who seemed to glow. *Who am I? Oh, this couldn't be... not Mary Smithers.*

Her mouth stirred into an incredulous smile that moved up into her hazel eyes. Turning, she held out her arms wide to see how those full sleeves on the purple blouse worked, then reached for her blow dryer and fixed her hair into the style it was meant to go in, softly falling towards her cheeks; only this time, she brushed one side of it back and curled it around her ear. *Hmmm, why not?*

Now, quickly, lest she lie down upon her bed again and give up this "dress-up" game, she rubbed on the free sample creams that Jolanda had given her – moisturizer, foundation, eye cream, then brushed rouge onto her cheeks and tapped on some soft gray/purple eye shadow. Jolanda had shown her how to do this once on a quiet afternoon; she'd practiced on her; and now she applied the eyeliner just the way she had done, and added a soft pink lipstick.

It's all pretend, isn't it? I don't have to go out. No, but this is a fun way to spend the evening.

Hand slipped into the small silver jewel box on her bureau, she found them. Yes, there they were; the ones he had given her so many years ago; those silver earrings with a slight drop, ones she never wore because they reminded her of him. Maybe she could just try them on...

Surveying herself once more, she was nearly dazzled by the sight of this woman in that mirror. An attractive woman in a long black skirt, a purple blouse and earthy cowboy boots stared back at her. Oh my! Oh, where had she been for so long?

"Mary! Mary come here..."

She glanced at her watch. 7:47.

She walked out of her bedroom and into the living room where she calmly took her mother's tray and started towards the kitchen.

Her mother squinted and removed her glasses.

"What on earth? What are you doing all painted up like that?"

She didn't answer, just continued to walk into the small adjacent kitchen.

"That new movie's on tonight you know... the one with Sean Connery and Richard what's his name. You're going to watch it with me aren't you? You promised."

Mary swallowed hard, walked back into the living room and faced her elderly mother lying there on the couch; waiting for her time to come. Yes, she'd promised. *But is that how life was supposed to be? Waiting around for death?* She kissed her on the forehead, strode into the hallway, put her pink scarf around her neck and slipped into her black rain coat. "No time to talk Mother. I'm going out..."

"What? I thought you were staying home and watching the movie with me.... Who with?"

"A friend. Don't wait up. I might be late."

"Well, I never.... It's supposed to be a good movie..."

Mary closed the door.

Gulping in the stale air, she walked along the corridor of old thinkers towards the elevator. Tonight, she had her own movie. Tonight, nothing could make her feel bad. And when Gordon's eyebrows rose up high at the sight of her and he leaned over and kissed her softly on her mouth, she smiled all over, remembering...Yes, she was more than a daughter; she was a woman – and going somewhere. It was okay to flush with joy and feel tremulous and excited. Tonight, she was *alive* again!

The End

A message from Melba . . .

I hope you enjoyed the stories in *Filled with Purple: Short Stories & Inspiration for Women*. If so, please watch for new books in the *Inspiration for Women Series*. They will be:

2. *Filled with Light: Miracles & Inspiration for Women* is a book filled with true stories of miracles and other inspiring experiences.

3. *Filled with Midlife Matters: Essays & Inspiration for Women*. Meditations and musings on such topics as creativity, reclaiming your vision, gratitude, trust, friends, and even Beethoven, will inspire you to reflect upon your own life.

4. *Filled with Hope: Stories of change & Inspiration for Women,* will inspire you to feel better about your own spiritual growth and all the twists and turns in your life.

5. *Filled with Magic: Stories & Inspiration for Women* will remind you of the magic in your own life. Child-like stories will make you laugh with the silliness of life.

You can reach Dr. Melba Burns by e-mail:
melbawrites@gmail.com
or visit www.melbaburns.com